CW00497158

This story is based on the life of red squirrels, ⟨ of engaging children whilst educating them endangered species.

After the story, there are some captivating photographs, and interesting squirrel facts to tell children.

Cover design and illustrations by Kate Northover

Photographs by Helen Butler

First published 2023 by Red Squirrel Enterprises

ISBN: 978-0-9552314-8-3

Many thanks to Island Biscuits who helped fund the production of this book

For more information on the Isle of Wight red squirrels, and to find out how you can help protect them, please visit:

www.wightsquirrelproject.co.uk   iowredsquirreltrust.co.uk

High in the treetops in the woods, a young red squirrel, Ginger was playing and having fun.

She had just finished a breakfast of nuts and berries and said goodbye to her mother.

She was leaving to find a home of her own. It would be an adventure.

Ginger knew she must find shelter before the cold night came.

She was very lucky and found a cosy hole in a tree where she would be safe and warm.

Ginger rose early the next morning and, feeling hungry, looked for some nuts to eat.

She was so busy she didn't notice the angry cry of the squirrel whose nuts she was eating.

The angry squirrel swished his tail with annoyance and told Ginger, 'Leave this wood, there is no room for you here!'

Ginger was very frightened and ran as fast as she could until she reached a road. She thought she should try to reach the other side of the road.

Ginger looked up and down the road for a safe place to cross and saw branches stretching across the road.

'That is a safe place to cross a road,' she said to herself.

Following the trees Ginger came to a large garden and sat in a tree looking about for some food and a drink.

She saw birds feeding and went to join them.

Next morning Ginger was up at daybreak and after a quick wash and scratch, ate breakfast.

A bowl of water on the lawn caught her eye and she jumped off the bird table to the lawn and ran across to drink.

As she drank, Ginger felt a grip on her tail and cried 'What has bitten my tail?' As she pulled away, a cat was left with a mouthful of hair.

Ginger ran to the nearest tree and climbed to the top. She was very frightened.

She raced through the tree tops until she came to a large beautiful wood.

'There is plenty of room for me here,' said Ginger happily as she leapt through the branches. 'I can make this wood my home.'

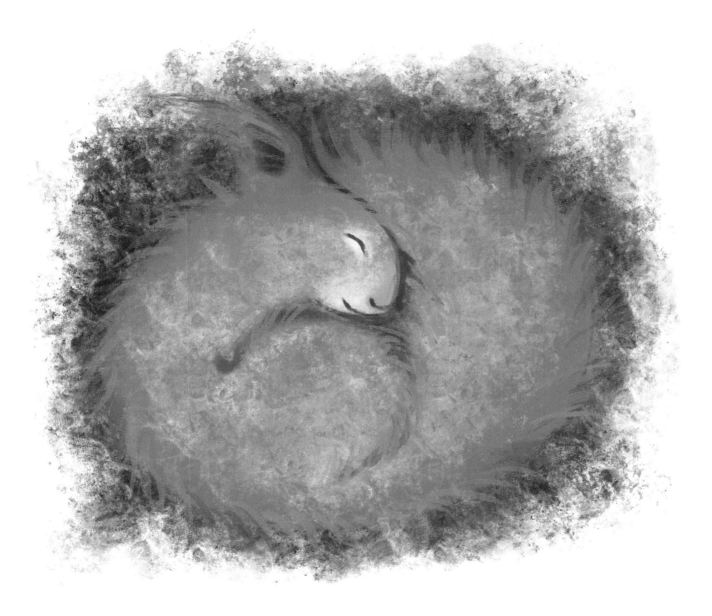

Feeling tired and hungry now, Ginger found a tree hollow to rest in.

She lined it with moss to make it cosy and warm.

Sometimes Ginger would run back through the trees to the garden to eat nuts. She was always careful to stay off the ground, away from the cat.

'I do enjoy teasing the cat,' she thought.

People loved to watch Ginger play and she scampered about just to make sure they didn't forget to leave her some nuts. Sometimes they would leave a juicy apple or a carrot as well.

Summer passed and autumn came again. There were a lot of nuts on the trees and Ginger busily gathered enough to eat and then safely buried the rest.

She would eat the nuts through the winter.

January came and Ginger was looking very pretty with her thick winter coat and long ear tufts. She decided to look for a friend.

She wandered through the trees and a squirrel started to chase her round and round the trees. Then another joined in later in the day.

'This is fun!' laughed Ginger. It was good to have friends to play with.

Late in March she had two baby squirrels of her own.

Baby squirrels are called kittens.

When they were born, the kittens did not have their pretty fur coats and their eyes were closed.

.A few weeks later, the kittens had grown a fine coat of hair and after four weeks they opened their eyes.

'Now I will have to think of names for them,' thought Ginger.
She looked at each kitten and thought hard.
'I will call you Rusty because of your red coat. You will be a very handsome boy.'

The other kitten was a girl and a very pretty dark red.
'I will name you Hazel,' she said as she proudly looked at her family.

When the two kittens reached three months old,
it was time to leave home.

Ginger was very sad but she knew they would have
lots of adventures before they found a home,
just as she had done.

Twelve interesting things to know about red squirrels

1. You cannot tell the difference between boys and girls by their size or colour

2. Red squirrels can be all sorts of colours – brown, red, ginger, nearly black or even grey

3. Red squirrels have ear tufts in the winter but not in the summer

4. Red squirrels live in trees and feel safe there. They eat nuts and seeds found in the trees

5. Red squirrels like to play with their brothers and sisters

6. A nest built on a branch is called a drey but a nest built in a tree hollow is called a den. It is very cosy and warm

7. A squirrel's back legs can turn so they can run down a tree as easily as they run up

8. Red squirrels are safer running in trees than running along the ground. They need high hedges and trees to use as 'squirrel roads' so they can safely travel between woods

9. Mother red squirrels raise their babies without help from father squirrel and the babies are called kittens

10. Red squirrels wave their tail very fast when they are angry

11. Red squirrels like a drink of water. They lap like a cat does

12. All squirrels bury food when there is more than they can eat, rather like people putting food in the larder